That Which Creeps

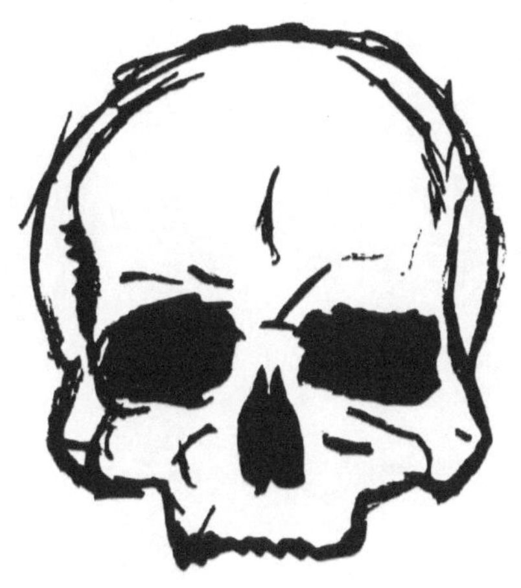

J.R. Packard

CONTENTS

Chapter 1

When The Cold Snow Descends

"I just don't know anymore, John. It'll surely break her heart once we tell her."

"It's a mutual agreement, Mary." John responded. "You can't say now, after all the finances have been squared away, that we'll undo the divorce. Lilly is finally old enough; sure, it won't strike a good spot within her, but she should understand."

John looked out the window of the small coffee shop on the outskirts of the high tree-laden mountains, giving a deep sigh of unhappiness at the attrition of his once fruitful marriage. Mary, meanwhile, could only stare down at her full mug and fail to enjoy the simple, pleasant aroma that the bean water gave off. Only the sight of Lilly far past the other side of the mountain passes could ease

her mind and inflict if not the smallest bit of reprieve from

stress.

     The state of what their relationship had become

was not due to one reason alone, nor was it necessarily a

founded growth of contempt each had for one another.

They had both been ruminating over it for a considerable

amount of time, since when Lilly (their daughter)

journeyed off to the university. The reasons were numbered;

each too petty to mention, yet a large culmination of them

all. It was, in fact, the last trip the couple would make before

parting ways: to see their child once more, breaking the

sorrowful news to her, before finally splitting ways.

     Despite the dull and low-some emotions of the

moment, they were, of course, very excited to see Lilly, who

had been away for the last year, and if it truly was John and

Mary's last moment together, they both felt it worthwhile.

"We best get a move on." Said John as he stood up. "Probably still about five hours left to go and God knows how much traffic we'll encounter once in Seattle."

They both left the check and made their way back to their small urban-fitting vehicle.

"Do you feel that too?" Asked Mary.

"It did get abnormally chilly, didn't it?" Said John as he looked up to the sky. "Good thing I brought a jacket."

The two then hopped in the vehicle, readying themselves for the long drive ahead and the even longer return. Mary, being the passenger, threw a blanket over her and covered her eyes in an attempt to sleep.

John turned on the radio, only to a slight degree so as not to wake her. As he found out, the air was becoming oddly cold for early September, but, as they were on the pass, he thought nothing of it and turned on the heater. With every five minute interval, he had to progressively turn the knob more and more until, to his bewilderment, it began to snow. It was at the same time that a deep fog began to settle on the ground and eventually engulf the car in a short time.

The shock—which was moreso confusion—grew to a point where he could no longer keep it contained and had to wake up Mary. She slowly opened her eyes until coming to her senses and leaning upright quickly.

"How weird." John said while they both half-laughed. "Snow doesn't usually start falling here at least until November. It was 80 degrees not three hours ago."

A few moments later, they heard what could only

have been a jet flying over in an unknown direction. This

too, did not seem very odd. Provided the weather, it'd only

make sense for the craft to return to the well-known nearby

base about 30 miles away into the valley below.

The snow and fog seemed to grow heavier with

each minute; so much so, that they considered turning back

and staying the night in the valley Eastward. Indeed, what

caught John's attention most was the lack of cars on the

road. At that time of the year, the road should have been

fairly filled, but it was as though they had all disappeared.

Even with the fog lights on, he forced himself to

slow to a meager four miles per hour. Obviously not ideal.

It was then that he approached a car on the side of

the road in the distance. As he got closer, he noticed the

doors open on it and felt he could provide some sort of

assistance, if needed. He parked alongside it to get a closer look but found no others which he thought was strange. After rolling down his window and yelling out to no avail, he slowly stepped out to find footprints going downhill. Wearing no more than tennis shoes, jeans, and a jacket, he wasn't prepared to go any further and expect what may have happened. Regardless, one could not have even seen three feet down into the slope because of the thickness of the mist.

It all unsettled John and he didn't know what to make of it. "Perhaps their car broke down." He thought. "But then again, why abandon it and not travel down the road to find some sort of help?"

He tried not to fill his mind with so many thoughts and returned to the car where he told Mary they broke down and went to find a passerby; likely, they'd walk a ways, seeing as there was no one else in sight.

They attempted to carry on up the highway but found it evermore difficult, laughing that they should have brought their truck instead. Even the air appeared to have changed. It felt more saturated somehow; as though there was more oxygen in it than normal.

"Do you think we should turn off?" Asked Mary, as they passed a small side road that led up to a group of cabins.

John ignored her for the most part, instead nibbling gently on his fingernails, concerned—not with the weather specifically, but how they'd find shelter if the weather kept its ungodly pace.

They must've traveled about an additional two miles before John relented and turned around. The car, at this time, was dangerously close to getting stuck and they could only guess how long they would have to live in their humble car before the roads cleared. They could only hope that one of the vacational cabins would take them in for the night.

The snow increased in strength with every passing second. By the time of the U-turn, a full-blown blizzard had essentially formed and they had to rely on memory of where to go. Mary brought out her cellphone to inform her daughter of the circumstances. Of course, it no longer worked, as didn't the car radio.

It was likely about eight minutes away in distance from the homes when the car's strength finally gave out and John and Mary found themselves stranded. The air grew cold so fast that the snow had no time to melt beforehand, and there was likewise little to no ice on the ground. Yet, the amount of snow (of which the uppermost part froze beneath the fog line) was just too much and overpowered the shrimp of a vehicle.

After countless attempts at freeing the wheels, John had to accept the fact that they weren't going anywhere. The thought crossed his mind of walking to the cabins, but there was no guarantee anyone would be there or let them in. The immediate thought, however, was to just stay put. John was an Eagle Scout and knew the workings in and out of survival. Rule one of being stranded is to stay put, and he was more than familiar with how to thrive in the cold—especially with the halfwit shelter of their small Subaru Sedan. Still, without any supplies other than a blanket, Fall clothes, a knife, and a workless cellphone, any amount of time in the vessel would be dire.

They ended up waiting for approximately two hours. About that time, the sun was beginning to set and, if they were indeed going to trek through the hazy blizzard up the small road, they were sure to do it soon. Grave worry set in thick and quick.

"What do you think we should do?" Asked Mary, shivering while covered in the blanket.

"We could stay;" replied John, "but there's no telling how long this weather will last: it could be days, a week even. Our tank is already half empty. I say we walk to the cabins. If we don't receive an answer or aren't welcome, then we come back and we're in the same spot as we were before. We may as well try something."

Mary nodded in approval.

They grabbed all they could out of the vehicle that they felt important: mainly the blanket, a pocket knife, snacks, and a backpack. From that point on—from the safety and refuge of the car that provided a semblance of escape—they'd have to endure the pain of what was to come—whatever that would be...

Without any sort of winter gear, and mere semi-post-summer attire in lieu, they found toil after only minutes of departing. It was near impossible to stay in any one direction amidst the incessant snow and four-foot layer of fog—let alone hone in on any destination. Still, they could see the dirt path below them faintly and, after a short while, finally the porch light of the nearest cabin uphill.

Upon reaching it, after what took far longer than it should've, they noticed two vehicles there; a good sign. The door was answered by a burly man in the likeness of Santa Clause, of all people. He was an older man with a white, lofty beard, beer belly, and overalls.

"Can I help you?" He asked in a quasi-annoyed manner.

"Our car has become stuck on the road and we were wondering if we could stay with you for a few hours and get out of this storm. Or try your phone at the very least." Asked John.

The elderly man looked quite displeased, as though he relished solitude and did not like company—even if given the chance to aid distressed individuals.

"I already let in another group. More the merrier, I suppose." He said with what seemed to be sarcasm.

"We really do appreciate it." Replied John, relieved they'd have a haven, if only temporarily, given the predominant evil breath of the wilderness outside.

They shut the door on the outside just as a massive wall of fog overcame the small stead. Within the living room they entered were two men and a woman. They all seemed very friendly and John and Mary got acquainted with them. The three were all friends on a celebratory road trip after they'd graduated from college. There was Pete, a handsome looking man with combed black hair, his girlfriend, Megan, and their long-time friend Rick. Pete was the most sociable of the three and he who seemed on top of everything with a level head. Rick and Megan showed worry and atypical fright. Of course, to be scared in the situation at hand would be only too natural, but their faces took that panic too far and they both sat on the couch immediately after shaking John's hand, likely to calm themselves.

Will, the owner of the cabin, then took the stage. He told everyone they could only stay the night unless the snow got worse. He was truly by definition a hermit and liked living alone, but didn't have the will to simply kick someone out into a raging blizzard for which they'd surely perish. He then laid out some ground rules of where people would sleep and instructed that no one touch his food without asking. Needless to say, he didn't enjoy visitors.

With that being said, Will appeared to have a good heart and under the depressing circumstances, he offered his large stash of alcohol to everyone. They stood outside not long after that, sipping rum, and discussing the strangeness that was upon them. For the most part, laughter filled the cold air. They were all more than positive that the snow was a freak of nature and it'd all blow over soon. They'd be mistaken.

Even as John laughed and doubted alongside them, he couldn't help but look outward into the mist and get an eerie feeling. He couldn't restrain his racing thoughts, being bothered and out of joint; he was unsettled for a reason not even he could pinpoint.

"I think I'll head in to warm up." He said, making an excuse to flee from the confounding murk.

The others joined him and they sat around for most of the night, giving their opinions on what was occurring and talking about their planned destinations. The friend group (Pete, Megan, and Rick) were from Idaho and making a trip to alaska. A long way for sure.

After Will had a good six shots in him, and after Pete inquired about all the alcohol, he admitted to them how he was somewhat of a loner and drunk for the past years after he lost his wife in a car accident. Sadder still, he hadn't had contact with his son or grandson since due to his whiskey. John felt bad for the man. He wasn't mean by any sense of the word, but rather stubborn not wanting them there. After the drinks, however, he seemed to lighten up.

Suddenly, the group began to get very cold and they noticed the gas had gone out. It was peculiar, but nothing to get disturbed over given the circumstances. Will had a back-up woodstove and a large stack of wood that could easily last them a month.

Most passed out in their stupor about three hours later. John and Mary were given a spot on the carpet with sleeping bags and lay beside one another. All was natural until, likely around midnight, John was awoken to a mysterious sound. At first, it was but a thud against the wall. He thought little of it—only that it was a branch blowing in the wind. As he rested and closed his eyes again, however, he was alarmed at the sound of a woman's voice outside crying for someone. It was faint; he was only able to make out that it was, in fact, a woman.

He went and grabbed a flashlight and shone it into the pitch blackness from outside the window. He was dumbfounded how anyone could possibly orient themselves in the darkness with the fog and snow. Still, he made an effort to examine but found nothing. John was an exceedingly generous and kind man and, in any other situation, would certainly have gone into the elements to help locate her, but, again, he got a terrible feeling in his gut that something was just not right. As difficult as it was, he decided to rest again and fall slowly asleep.

Chapter 2

That Which Creeps

John, having difficulties dreaming throughout the night, was the first to awake; part of it may also have been for the fact that he drank the least out of everyone the night before.

His first instinct was to check on the matter outside. To his disappointment, things had not turned for the better. The snow level had grown to at least two feet while the fog was even thicker than before—which says a great deal.

He put on his inadequate snows and stepped out on the porch for a late dawn cigarette. As he leaned against the wood slabs of the front wall, he caught sight of weird footprints about ten feet in the distance. They were queer and not from any sort of animal he had ever heard of. He chose to walk along them for only a moment to find, to his surprise, they stopped; right there in the open, in no normal place. It was out of the question that the snow covered up the remaining ones. It'd elude the mind to think the rest would be covered also and unexpectedly cease with after one solid print. They appeared to have been from large webbed duck feet, about eight inches across. There were also even larger claws marks that extended from the toes. It only makes sense for a creature to need webbed feet to walk on snow, but, then again, snow was not usual. Very strange.

It was then that he looked up after acknowledging the stronger wind. Above, in the sky, was something like a gigantic swirl—like the eye of a hurricane. After examining it further, one may have considered it as almost a portal. That thought was ridiculous, of course. Fog spued downward from its (seemingly) entrance or center, as well as equally odd birds. They appeared large; duck-sized perhaps, but had no feathers.

John could only observe in amazement at the impossible sight and assume his knowledge of the sciences were smaller than he once thought.

As bewildering as it was, that was not the most eeriest and confusing part. There seemed to be two very dim and faint suns in the sky. One could liken them unto two bright moons in the hardly light morning that he was in. It was this that sounded the alarm of panic the most, yet he still tried to rationalize it as simply an optical illusion.

His immediate inclination was to get and show the others, not being able to contain the wonder and fright. As they all stood outside and saw the phenomenon together, they, instead of losing control of their mouths, kept them agape and looked in silence.

"It must be some Winter hurricane." Said Pete.

"Those exist?" Replied Rick.

Pete only glanced at him, being unsure and perhaps trying to comfort himself by thinking it was all natural.

"We best get back in." John commented. "Who knows what more will come out of that thing."

As they sat inside and cooked breakfast, Will went to the back of the house to grab firewood. As he turned around with a good stack in his arms, he noticed a strange blackish-grey mold growing against the outer wall, nearby trees, and some pieces of old wood. Living in the forest, he was most accustomed to identifying various fungi, but this type was unknown, distinct, and different. It bubbled as though it was boiling, and spread fast enough to be seen with the naked eye.

He put his head close to it—not to touch, but only to get a better look. He immediately began coughing and nearly choking off the fumes it gave out. After receding away from it, the coughing stopped and Will was about to go back inside, ignoring the spreading poison. However, as he opened the door, he heard a voice call his name from behind him.

It was a man's voice whom he could not identify and its origin was somewhere deep in the outer fog. Will yelled out, "Hello?", but no reply returned. He, unlike John, was not as brave. He felt something was wrong and hurried inside, choosing not to mention the happening, thinking he may have been hallucinating or mistaking noises.

After breakfast, the group had begun to unexpectedly bicker. None wanted to stay—with Will being the most adamant about them lingering. Rick, Pete, and Megan, were the most serious. Their plans were being cut short and, if they did not get a move on, their trip would end, be ruined, due to going back to their respected jobs. John and Mary felt the same way, but tried to persuade them otherwise. Both knew it would be unquestionably stupid and foolish to try to go anywhere; that is, give they could in the first place.

Even Will gave his two cents that leaving when things were getting evermore terrible was pure idiocy.

"Fine." Said Megan: the one most irritated.

It was at that exact moment that they heard a terrifying, petrifying sound. It was like a high-pitched, deep roar that reverberated off the walls. They shut their mouths at once and looked through the windows, but failed to see

anything. The ground then shook as though a small

earthquake was bashing beneath their feet, but more so of a

giant walking. Will's German Shepherd began barking

loudly at the door and they were forced to silence him the

best they could. Powerless to the mysterious entity that

could only be compared to a dinosaur, they dimmed the

lights and hid. Branches could be heard breaking and trees

falling. As quickly as it came, did it evaporate into

nothingness.

"What the hell was that?" Whispered Pete as he

arose from behind a couch.

Will immediately went to get his hunting rifle.

"Whatever it is," he said, "it's not natural and

dangerous."

The group immediately and positively knew something was wrong. There was no "hurricane" and they wanted nothing to do with whatever creeping thing lay beyond the fog. No imaginable creature could produce such antics.

Oddly, each person said little and kept their opinions to themselves. They may have been too scared to discuss and decipher the potential peril. Each subgroup talked amongst themselves: John with Mary; Pete with Megan and Rick; and Will sitting silently after grabbing a whiskey bottle, with his gun held tightly. A crowbar could not separate the weapon from his grip.

"I no longer feel safe." Mary said in John's ear.

"Maybe it was thunder or a military weapon from down in the valley. We shouldn't jump to hair-raising conclusions." John exclaimed to the group.

"Maybe he's right." Said Pete. "Let's just relax. We have a gun; we're protected."

The two seemed to quell the fear and all went for the alcohol to calm their nerves. Talk and jokes were had with them pretending they were fine. They weren't, but kept it inward.

Approximately seven hours passed, until they heard a truck approaching down the road with its fog lights on. It then unexpectedly stopped. They figured it must've gotten stuck in the two-and-a-half feet of snow.

Reluctantly, John took up the most courage and went a little ways outside to take a better look while the others watched from inside.

He saw indistinctly a man open the door and wave at him so as to get his attention. He was indeed stuck and needed help.

At this time, the wind, fog, and blizzard was getting even worse and there showed no sign of stopping. The foreign man would have no chance of making it anywhere, even if the car was freed, so John knew he'd have to take him in.

They tried yelling at each other, but the sound was far too muddled to make out a single word. John slowly began to walk towards him when, out of the treeline ran an ill-defined creature towards the truck. John instantly stood in his tracks, heart beating fast, as he saw the being tear into the man and haul him off into the woods. All he heard was a yell only known in Hell.

Without thinking, he sprinted as fast as he could into the cabin and slammed the door.

"Lock everything! Barricade the windows and doors!" He cried to the group.

"What happened!?" Said everyone, nervously and frit.

"Just trust me! There's something out there that killed the driver."

Without hesitation, the group accepted the command and ripped wood from anywhere they could, beginning to nail any and all exits shut.

"What the hell happened!?" Demanded Will to John.

"I saw the driver being taken by something in the blizzard. I couldn't make out its features—only that it wasn't a normal animal."

Will, with a straight, low-hanging face, said nothing, went over to the door and fired three rounds into the cold air, presumably to ward off whatever was out there.

"Now listen." He said, turning around to a silent crowd. "Whatever John saw is now irrelevant. We got bigger things to worry about and, regardless of that 'thing', no one's going anywhere any time soon. We got to worry about the affairs inside first. Starvation? Hypothermia? That'll kill us first and we have to keep our heads straight. This is my place and I'm not letting anyone or thing in."

Most nodded at him and the rest obviously agreed. Will may very well have been a hardened, strict, and even slightly inconsiderate man at times, but he was right. Only

John knew what he saw (which was hardly anything), so the group had to take his word. It was for this reason that John attempted not to freak out or overly terrify them and send them into a spiraling bout of trepidation. He made it clear the being was not friendly, likely not an animal, and they'd do best to hunker down, but elaborated no more than that.

Every person took a checkpoint, either at a window or a door. Minutes turned into hours which culminated in half a day's time of waiting while all stood still, calm, and quiet; there was nothing. About then, all had fallen asleep, save John and Mary who stood by the kitchen window, looking out for whatever they could unfortunately find.

"What did you see?" She said. "We've been locked up in lies for the last year. I need you to tell me the truth."

"Mary, the truth is that I don't know what I saw. I couldn't get a proper look at what that creature was, but it curdled my blood. I can't get the man's screams out of my head. We'll be okay; just got to stay put."

"I think they're beginning to respect you." Said Mary. "You're the one taking the most responsibility and keeping order."

"I don't know about that." He responded. "It's been a decade but I'm an Eagle Scout and was in bootcamp. I had to function under pressure. A hermit and college kids: they can't take care of themselves like they should in this situation. I'm no leader but am probably the most senseful."

Then, suddenly out of nowhere, the dead, skinned driver flew from out of the blinding snow against the window—leaving a spill of blood on the glass. The two nearly fell to the floor in shock and horror.

As they arose, they could see two bodiless neon red eyes staring at them through the fog about 50 feet away high in the trees. They were being watched and stalked.

With no other humans for tens of miles, it was understandable why they were prime targets. Yet, at the same time, it was not clear. Did he/they want food? Shelter? Warmth? The questions were infinite. The only answer they had was that they could not leave; not in any conceivable way, at least.

The former couple chose to keep the incident to themselves. All were already aware there was something lurking in the blizzard—something foreboding—and they didn't need to scare them more.

To get their minds off of everything, they all decided to make clothes out of blankets and snowshoes out of boards. If, in the incredible future, they did have to leave, they'd need means. Spears were also fashioned out of knives and table legs. It would be a stretch to call them adequate weapons, but they were better than nothing.

Over the course of the next two days, Rick had begun to get more impatient and showed signs of suffering from cabin fever. He'd talk to himself, whisper nonsense under his breath, and lash out over the smallest inconveniences. Everyone worried about him but didn't know what to do.

He'd propose over and over again, to the point of annoyance, how he wanted to try and make it to the truck. He was confident he could get the vehicle unstuck and once on the road, "make it to safety"--wherever that was.

Naturally, the group refused tirelessly, but fear grew that he'd do something reckless or stupid like eating all the food or even harming one of them out of isolated madness.

"Do you want to be trapped forever? We'll die in this prison of our own making. Come with me or let me go. I don't care, but I must leave; I can no longer endure this. The lights are still on in the truck. I can follow them and make it. Give me the gun and I'll be fine."

"I'll be damned before I give it to you." Said Will with a stern voice.

"Fine. The spears should suffice." Said Rick.

"Let me go! Set me free!" He cried.

Finally, after a preposterous amount of pleading with him, they finally decided to let him try. It was a hard pill to swallow, but there was no stopping him. Surely, in the middle of the night he'd sneak out anyways—breaking through the door and endangering them all as they slept.

They fitted him with a makeshift pair of snowshoes, a spear, and a small sack of food, provided he did succeed. It would happen that night when noises seemed to dull. Whatever was out there could surely see in the night with their/its glowing eyes, but with the fog, snow, and darkness combined, it set humans more at ease and feel cloaked—even if that was not true.

His college colleagues gave him a tight hug with tears from Megan before he departed and the door was quickly barricaded behind him. His movements were semi-fast and he made sure to keep his careful movements silent. He also journeyed without a light source for extra cover. If he had to run in any direction other than the car or cabin, he'd be lost in the blackness.

To everyone's surprise, as they watched through the cracks in the windows, he made it to the truck.

As Rick approached and found the driver's door opened, he heard a voice emanating from the backside. It was of a baby crying and he couldn't utterly fathom how that was possible.

His excitement then swiftly turned and he knew something was wrong. He started to move his feet again when a sound of a woman cried out in some unknown direction, "Help us.".

Where she was was unknown. The baby was definitely under the vehicle. He got about arm's length to it, about to bend down, when he was suddenly grabbed by the feet and thrown under the truck. A scream lasting only one second was heard until nothing.

The others could only watch and bury their faces against one another—both fearful and terror-stricken. They would never leave again, they thought. Or would they? The car would thereby be off limits. At any rate, the snow was piling up: at least three feet and continuing upwards. If any more attempts at escape were possible, time was running out.

"Calm down!" Exclaimed John as they panicked hysterically. "We have to think rationally. First thing we do is ration resources. Food and wood are the number one priorities. Water is easy; we can always melt snow. If worse comes to worse, we'll burn what we can from inside. This weather can still pass. The wind, snow, and fog may dissipate at any moment; it's only been a few days."

As they stood, Megan faced the window and noticed the mysterious creature (perhaps a different one), looking onward through the fog. It was the first time they could fully see it in all of its features.

It looked exceedingly and thickly scaled—almost like a reptilian standing upright. It was human in nature, but at least eight feet high. One could see its large eyes, its fanged teeth sticking through its lips, massive claws hanging down, and webbed, sharp "feet".

It looked like a contradiction and conundrum. Scaled? Would that mean it's cold-blooded? How on Earth could it survive in the cold?

"Maybe its blood is different." Said Pete. "Like a bee with a sort of antifreeze in it.".

Suddenly the being ran as fast as it could to the home when, out of nowhere, a gigantic, impossible claw appeared through the sky, grabbed it, and threw it into the woods. There was no shown body; only the sharp claw that must've weighed 500 pounds. Whatever it was, it was definitely stronger and seemed to eat the relatively small creature which gave out a high-pitched shriek.

The lights then went out. It could've possibly had something to do with the entity outside, but it was more probable that it was coincidentally the snow. It may have been a good thing, as they didn't want to be seen. They used candles, flashlights, and lamps from then on.

Nothing could be said for the rest of the night. They sat around each other with a candle dimly burning on the center coffee table, wrapped up in blankets. Only Pete opened his mouth to no replies.

"How much longer can this weather last? What is this fog?"

Chapter 3

A Perilous Proposition

"John, why don't you go down to get some canned fruits." Asked Will.

John was more than happy to go down into the cellar. The entrance was from the inside and nothing could possibly have been down there, with it being underground and having no exits. There was nothing to be afraid of.

As John descended the darkness of the stairs with his flashlight, he became uneased. "They're just stairs.". He thought. "Why do my bowels quake?".

There was something about it, for whatever reason. Walking down into an abyss of blackness and cold air alone. What lay outside had begun to stretch his mind in all directions and he no longer felt the slightest sense of safety anywhere he went; even within the home. He was the most level-headed one, but no mind is impenetrable. He knew he'd have to get a grip and not start to succumb like the others.

He came up with only a handful of jars. There were about three left down there that he chose not to mention to the rest. Food was already running dangerously low and he'd have to forcefully ration it himself if worse came to worse.

"I have an idea." Pete said to John. "Maybe we should try going to another cabin; just the two of us."

"Are you crazy!?" Exclaimed Megan. "Have your eyes been closed the whole time? There's no way you'd make it."

"The cabin is not far at all. It's closer than the truck and in the open, not too near the pine trees. We have to get supplies and food. If not, we'll all die of starvation. You know it just as well as I do. Now's the best time while we still have our strength."

The group couldn't argue, as much as they wanted to. Pete was right. One or two lives gone (if that were to happen) would be better than all of them perishing.

"Let's think of the alternatives." Said Mary.

They all thought deeply but to no avail.

"As much as I hate it, he's right, Mary." Said John. "It's a stupid thing to do. *Really* stupid, but we *will* die unless we do it. Do you want to eat the dog?"

"The hell with that!" Yelled Will.

"Then that's that." Said Pete. "Do you want to come, John? The more hands the better. We need to grab as much as we can so a second trip isn't needed."

Mary tried her utmost to dissuade John, but he wouldn't budge. His bravery was too great and his selflessness and logic got the best of him.

"I'll go." He said.

The two men went to get snowshoes and makeshift spears. They asked for Will's rifle but he wouldn't relent. He'd die before someone took it away.

Megan was both sad and furious, but mostly the latter. She loathed him going and showed stark disapproval of it, not fully grasping that it was utterly necessary. Both her and Pete would die if they didn't go. Pete knew there was no consoling her and she wouldn't understand, but he did.

"I'm so sorry, John." Said Mary. "The divorce was a mistake, even if it doesn't matter now. I love you and you know how much I hate this, but you've always been iron-headed. Promise you'll be smart and careful."

"I will." He responded, kissing her.

John went to get a long rope. We'll tie ourselves to the cabin so we can find our way back. It'd be impossible to do so in this weather.

Again, they took the boards off the door, preparing to instantly lock it up once they left. The two men looked at each other before leaving, both silently scared. Pete nodded at John and it was time.

Unlike Rick, they didn't want to walk slowly. It was still light out and they could see at least half-decently. They didn't run, but speed walked as fast as they could, making sure to stay shoulder-to-shoulder.

"Do you see that?" John asked.

About 12 feet ahead was the silhouette of a dog. As they got near, they found it was a pack of wolves; around seven. Their guts were torn out and seemed eaten. Most disturbingly, they had been skinned and their heads were missing.

The strange featherless birds were walking around them and pecking at their flesh. Their beaks were abnormally long for their sizes and were serrated deeply.

As they stood, looking with pure dread, they heard a tree fall from around a football field's length away. At the same time, they were overpowered by an exceedingly strong and gross smell of musk. God only knew what it was from and where it originated. Only one thing was on their minds: leave.

They began to finally run and came upon the nearest cabin in not too long. Quickly, they broke in and barricaded the door as before. The first went to the kitchen and were delighted to find each pantry filled to the brim with imperishable foodstuffs. They proceeded to essentially pig-out and fill their stomachs 'til they hurt.

They were well aware, unfortunately, that it was impossible to carry even a third of all the food with only two day backpacks. Their best bet and ideal situation would have been for all of them to journey there, but that was obviously out of the question. There was too much peril as it was for the two men, and the others would have rather died in Will's house than leave—even if death was sure to come in their cage of wood.

Afterwards, Pete and John felt it best to spend the night. It would worry Megan and Mary, but giving time to let whatever was outside leave (if there was something) was the best option.

Night soon fell and lightning struck outside. It was the most eerie night so far and definitely the most fear-induced, with the windows not being blocked. They could only keep their mouths shut, fall asleep quickly, and head out as soon as the sun arose.

Chapter 4

Megan's Madness

It was in the early morning when Mary awoke. She slept only approximately two hours, unable to experience any restful relief; nightmares and sweat composed her aura as each hour passed in the cold and dark.

She immediately went to the attic, ignoring her hunger pangs and weakness due to it. She sat beside the small window and looked out attentively into the blizzard and fog in great hopes that she'd see John's face appear. She knew it'd be nearly impossible to catch an eye of them from any meaningful distance but still, it was all she could do and wasn't about to give up hope so soon.

Meanwhile, below, Megan had secluded and confined herself in a corner. She sat on a chair facing the wall, as though one going through a major depressive episode would do. Unbeknownst to the others (besides Pete), she suffered various derailing mental disorders and took a cocktail of medications. She was frequented by serious depression and panic attacks. Her not having the medications certainly would have been worrisome and likely horrendous for her. Coupled with Pete and Rick being gone, only she knew how she felt.

Even in the relatively short time period in which Pete was gone, Mary and Will had started to heavily worry about her. Will and Mary were discussing the two men when, out of nowhere, Megan leapt out of her and began screaming that she "can't take it!".

She too-swiftly began throwing blankets and empty cans everywhere in order to find snowshoes and a better coat.

Mary and Will sprung up and yelled at her to calm down but their words seemed to have no effect.

"They're killing me! I have to find Pete!" She screamed.

"Shut up!" Yelled Will at her. "You're going to draw attention."

It was all fruitless. She was having a panic attack and would attract whatever lay outside if she didn't soon quiet down.

She got her shoes on but only managed to wrap herself in a blanket. She then threw a knife out of the drawer and put it between her belt.

"Megan, relax." Mary pleaded. "Don't be an idiot; they'll return. I care just as much about John as you do about Pete. You going out won't do any good—whether safe

or not."

"No! They're out there and need help. I can sense it.

We're being hunted and they'll get to Pete!"

Megan then grabbed a hammer and hit the door as

hard as she could.

"Let me the hell out of here!" She cried.

Finally, Will had enough of it. "If you want to kill

yourself then go for it, but don't drag us down with you."

He helped take the boards down for yet another

time and she ran out in an instant. Without any sort of

hesitation, she faded into the fog.

The wind had sped up to about 50 miles-per-hour, with the temperature being likely around 8 degrees. Both Mary and Will knew she wouldn't make it. Her only silver lining was making it to the other cabin, but without a rope or compass, she stood little chance. They wouldn't know what or how to tell Pete; that is, if he returned...

Chapter 5

Trapped

It was a little later, in the evening, when John and Pete sat in the other cabin, ruminating on leaving–knowing they had to, but still shaken and scared from the scene of the wolves. What would become of them? Safety? If only. They thought. They'd rather commit suicide than suffer the same fate as the poor canines.

It was that, the longer they stayed there, the more likely they'd be discovered; and, regardless, they'd eventually be snowed in. Pete also could never let go of the thought of never seeing Megan again; no, they'd leave, and soon for that matter.

They both felt it best to ransack the home one last time for anything useful–particularly weapons, but they could only dream. They parted ways and Pete went into the garage. To his disbelief, he found a seemingly working snowmobile. Naturally, he grew extremely elated, but the entrance was covered in feets of snow, and there was no hope of using the equipment without work. He grabbed a shovel and dug away as much as he could when he heard John loudly call his name.

John had been examining the backyard and came upon a dead man (presumably the owner) half-buried in the snow. Like the wolves, he was skinned and disemboweled. He held a large buck knife in his right hand which oddly had black blood on the blade. The body looked fresh; too fresh, and he knew he had died only a day before and not too long before the two men had arrived. There was an ax not far from him caught in a tree stump. John figured the man had gone out to grab it when the evil deed took place.

Pete rushed over as fast as he could. The two were at a loss for words.

"We have to leave. Now." Said Pete, breaking the silence. "I found a snowmobile. We can use it, but it'd be impossible to take everyone."

John was quick to grab the ax and they immediately went to follow the rope tied against the cabin. They had followed it for a good distance, when it unexpectedly stopped. It had apparently been cut and the remaining line was nowhere to be seen. To make it worse, their tracks from before were completely covered over and indiscernible. Only two choices were left: power on and hope to make it back to the others and risk getting lost, or return and live together, alone and with greater solitude.

The two men agreed that they'd press on. Their pace was not fast at first but, once they began to see humanoid shadows walking around, their confusion and disorientation meld with panic. Then, from behind them, came an inconceivable loud roar. It sounded almost like a bomb. There was no time left to think critically where they stepped. Run, run, was all there was on their minds. As they did, a smell of musk again hung in the air. John, for whatever reason—perhaps out of curiosity or to gauge the beast's distance—looked behind him, nearly stumbling to his feet. For the first time, he saw the large being. It was a giant that alternated walking on two feet and four. It had a beak-like snout that must've protruded fifteen feet outward with large teeth hanging around it. There were long horns on it, three in number. It had claws (like the one they saw before) similar to a crab's.

Despite its menacing appearance, it actually didn't seem to care about them. It was almost like it was warding them off and trying to frighten them, having suddenly stopped not too far away. Nevertheless, John and Pete were not the slightest bit ready to stop.

What could only have been described as a godsend, the men ran right into the original cabin, thanking the gods for their charity.

"Let us in! Let us in!" They demanded.

Mary and Will were awestruck at the fact that they had made it back alive and better yet, with droves of food (that would sadly not last long). John ran and threw his arms around his wife, as she cried in joy.

"Where's Megan?" Pete asked.

Mary and Will simply looked at one another. They didn't know how to explain that she essentially went out to commit suicide; given she never met up with them, the worst almost certainly turned out to be true.

"She went to find you, kid." Said Will in a deep voice.

"What!? How could you let her do that? I got to go back out!" Exclaimed Pete.

"She was distraught." Mary responded. "We couldn't hold her back. Everyone is staying put from now on—no more stupidity."

Pete, like Megan before, would not relent—even to logic. He went straight for the door when John blocked his path.

"Move it!" Pete commanded.

"We're not losing anyone else." Said John. "Look, I know how you feel. I do, but you're doing no one good going out there. You're staying."

Pete then raised his fist to hit John and pushed against him, but John was ready, deterred the punch, and knocked Pete to the ground.

"You're staying!" John yelled. "We all are..."

Pete managed to calm down a few moments later, but he was no less fraught. He and John rested on the couch, holding warm coffee with blankets draped over them. Mary and Will meanwhile went to look through the finds. Then, there came a knock.

"Megan?" Asked Pete, with a confused expression.

There seemed to be neither rush nor distress at the door, just one gentle knock after the other. Mary went and looked through the window. "It is her?" She said with an addled face.

"Megan!" Said Pete, as he jumped up and ran to the door. Once opened, he found her in a strange state. She didn't seem to have suffered any—even the smallest—sort of damage or wear from the weather, despite being gone so long. Pete could also not but notice her eyes: they were a lot darker than before. Her iris was pitch black and locating a pupil was impossible.

"What happened to your eyes?" He asked.

"It's from being off of my medication. It's just a side effect and has happened before."

Pete didn't know what to say to this but, no matter, he was more than pleased seeing her.

"I found a large house not far from here;" she said, once entered, "about 30 miles away."

"30 miles? Are you joking?" Said Will. "Bless you to think that's close."

"That's 60 miles you walked then." Commented John. "How is that possible? Even if I were walking on cement, I couldn't make that journey in such a short time. And why didn't you bring anything back with you?"

"Are you calling her a liar?" Asked Pete with an angry expression. "She's small. Obviously she couldn't bring anything back with her through the rugged landscape."

John said nothing further; yet, he could only remain perplexed. Why didn't she have frostbite? What happened to her eyes? He thought.

Megan went to sit by the stove at Pete's behest. She looked neither at the stove nor the rest, oddly. She stared only at the wall above it—almost in a trance. The others unspokenly agreed to drop any mention of her surviving, lest they endure the newfound wrath of Pete.

It was a day later when another knock came from the door. This one was far more mysterious and each person almost fell off the chairs in disbelief. Megan's survival was a hard enough pill to swallow as it was, but another?

"Answer it!" Yelled Megan. "Maybe it's help."

"Wait," Said Mary, "what if it's one of those things?"

"They'd just knock on the door?" Said Pete.

Again, they went to the window to see it was but a man. They agreed to let him in but give him a lot of attention.

"Hello." Said the man in a dull expression.

"Hi?" Said the rest all in sync.

"I was riding my bike when I was caught in this damned storm. I can't believe I managed to find someone. I should be dead."

Grasping Megan's survival was easier. How on Earth did he make it for so long; especially with the creatures outside? He looked funny, wearing a professional black business suit. He also had a strange, unidentifiable accent that they'd never heard before. Those were the least surprising features. He had no hair anywhere. Even his eyebrows and eyelashes were missing. He had tiny, pitch black eyes like Megan, and very thin lips.

He called himself Joe and seemed very friendly, but said little in the way of conversation. Each in the group were hesitant to let him in, but all were afraid to say their worries amidst the others, so they invited him in.

"Can't believe it's snowed this much." He laughed as he took his coat off. "Guess I'll get to ski early this year."

Besides him, the room was dead silent with all eyes his way. How could he be so lame? It was all like a joke to him and he was entirely oblivious to the dangers.

"Do you not know the *things* walking out there?" Asked Will.

"Things?" Joe asked.

"These creatures! It's amazing you haven't been killed!" Said John.

"Creatures? I'll guess we'll have to stay safe then... We'll be okay." Replied Joe, very nonchalant. "In that case, it's good to see humans amidst all of this."

"I was telling the others about a safehouse near here." Said Megan to him.

"I've heard of that house too!" Replied Joe. "It's about 15 miles away. It may be a better option."

"15? Why did you say 30?" Will inquired Megan.

"Leave her alone." Said Pete. "She got confused. Why would she lie?"

"Anyways, if that's the plan, we should all go–together. Safety in numbers." Said Joe.

"Just sit down," Said John to Joe. "and have some coffee. We'll need time to think about it."

"Time's shrinking." Joe commented.

Another day passed and John noticed the quietness of both Joe and Megan. Joe was the mystery man of them, so he had no way to know how he normally acted, but Megan had been far more talkative before she left outside. Still, with no real explanation, he assumed it to be fright or trauma.

Food was now running dangerously low—even after the rations Pete and John brought with them.

"What are you fixing yourself there?" Asked Mary as she ate a jar of jam with a spoon.

"Mustard with crackers." Laughed John.

Likewise, the others feasted on gravy mix, cake mix, and dried tomatoes.

"I'm going to take watch." Said John, as he grabbed a whiskey bottle and Will's rifle.

He went to the attic to peer out its small window in order to get a better look outside (which didn't mean much with the fog and constant pouring of snow). The snow had risen to about seven feet and they were no longer able to look through the windows.

About two hours later, he was well liquored-up, drunk, and had a stomach full of dog food. Everyone had, for the most part, become alcoholics at this time—which was understandable. It was all uneventful, until John glanced once more out the window after taking a swig, and saw two glowing eyes in a tree about 100-feet away.

It was high, but not one of the giant beings; its eyes were far too small and close. John stood at the edge of his seat and could only look at it. It seemed to be purposefully staring at him and John became unnerved. He felt as though the creature was somehow reading his mind and hypnotizing him. Then, nothing. The eyes shut and it disappeared.

Meanwhile, Pete was in the bathroom washing his hands when he looked in the mirror and was hurdled back. He saw his eyes had become pure black—even more so than

Joe and Megan's. He lifted back up to his feet only to find them normal once again. Nothing was wrong; nothing was inside, he thought. But, something bad, something sinister, was infiltrating. What was it infiltrating exactly? Only he could guess...

Chapter 6

Who Are You, Joe?

John remained in the attic throughout the night, then unexpectedly awoken around one in the morning. His head ached from the booze and he wished to fall back into his slumber, but was immediately turned on edge when he heard what could only be described as footsteps walking on the roof above him.

He nearly fell off his seat when he lunged at the window to see footprints heading straight for the cabin that stopped right in front of the wall. It was as though the creature leapt straight onto the home without alternating its course. They were as he saw them before: large, webbed, and with claw marks. The being(s) must have been extraordinary jumpers, which made perfect sense if they could be seen in the trees.

He then noticed the truck in the far distance. Only the faint glow of the lights were apparent; the body of it could not be seen. Oddly, the car's emergency lights were on and the headlights flickered or turned off and on three times after each passing five seconds. Having been a boy scout, he knew it was a signal of distress, but wouldn't be fooled. There was no way a person could have been out there and, if they were, they should've been dead.

The realization then came to him that whatever was out there was trying to lure them out. But why? He thought. What use did they have with humans?

As contradictory as it was—that is, wanting to keep guard but also wanting to sleep with Mary and ease the tension in his mind—he chose the latter and abandoned his post of being the lookout.

As he came down the ladder, he noticed a freezing cold breeze come from down the hall. In an instant, he ran to find the source, fearing something or someone had broken in. To his bewilderment, it was Joe. The glass of a window was broken from the other side of the boards and Joe was mindlessly staring out of it.

"What the hell are you doing!?" Yelled John.

"It was stuffy in here. The cabin needed some air." He replied.

"Are you crazy? Get away from there."

"Suit yourself." Said Joe, as he walked away to go lie down.

John was shocked at how on Earth the man would think such a thing. He knew he'd have to keep an even keener eye on him and would tell the group to do so as well

in the morning.

John couldn't sleep the rest of the night. It was a

combination of a hangover, fear of the eyes outside, and

worrying of Joe. He didn't trust him, and hadn't from the

start. There was something about him: perhaps his

appearance, or his relaxed, indifferent demeanor towards

their situation.

The morning proved to increase these thoughts.

Right at the get-go of everyone waking up, he insisted they

leave right away. Over and over, he'd try talking them into it.

Indeed, it was true that they were getting

desperate—particularly for food, and they did almost

certainly need to eventually leave, but reluctance obviously

clouded their minds after the deaths they had witnessed.

Peculiarly, Megan backed him up everytime he spoke, which was odd, since she was becoming increasingly mute. Pete had finally reunited with her and surely she didn't want to leave again after all the stories. Yet, she did somehow manage to return unharmed, and this, although unbelievable, was a persuading matter.

It just so happened to be then, as Joe spoke, that John asked about his foreign, unidentifiable accent.

"I'm from "Kopil." He said. "Not far from here."

Everyone looked at each other with confused faces. They all lived at least far in the vicinity of the city in the valley below, and had never heard of a "Kopil". Joe explained that it was but a place town, little-known to outsiders. They all believed him.

"Why don't you have any hair?" John asked.

"It's simply a combination of genetics and getting old." Replied Joe.

Again, the group took his word, having no other explanation. John was no doctor or biologist, but he couldn't fathom some form of deformity that would cause him to look as he did. He'd never even heard of people accidentally being born with black eyes. At any rate, he kept it in the back of his mind, but soon dismissed any thoughts of doubt that the man was telling the truth.

A little later, they were all sitting around the woodstove when John again caught an unconventional sight of Joe. The mysterious man was sitting in the corner of the room, just staring blankly at a wall. All were covered in blankets, save him, who still wore his inappropriate business dress.

"Are you not cold?" Asked John.

"I run warm." Replied Joe, still staring at the wall and not moving his head an inch. "Quite fortunate in this weather."

John became increasingly on guard with Joe, suspecting that there was something wrong and off about him, but he didn't know what. The same behavior was being shown by Megan, and the only explanation he had was that it was all due to stress and literal cabin fever.

After a half an hour, Will was in the kitchen and John took his chance to speak with him in private.

"I don't trust this man." Whispered John.

"You and me both." Said Will.

"I'm doubting that Kopil is even a place. I've lived here my whole life. I would have at least heard the name once." Said John. "He's lying at a minimum."

"What about his appearance? If you're right, and he's lying, how are we to trust him about that?" Will whispered, while looking in Joe's direction, who was still looking onwards at the wall.

"What do you make of all this?" Asked John. "Are we in some type of alternative world or dimension? How is all of this happening? Say I'm right about the alternative world theory, that could explain Joe's origins. But why doesn't he look like those creatures? And why hasn't he been attacked? Something about that "safehouse" also raises suspicion. What if Joe is somehow connected to *them*; as though they'd take over the bodies of humans—which he may have once been?"

"Straighten up, John. Don't start going looney, losing your mind, and coming up with ridiculous theories. We have no way of knowing and best leave it at that. You and I are dealing with this better than anyone; we can't lose our heads now when we most need them."

"Well, regardless, we can't turn our backs on him. If he gets out of line once, we throw him out. Agreed?" Said John.

Before Will could reply, they found Joe surprising them from behind.

"How much food is left?" Joe asked.

Swiftly taken aback and piqued, Will simply said, "Enough!", while giving Joe a stern face of disapproval.

"Whatever you say…" Said Joe, half-grinning as he walked away.

Will and John were to continue their conversation when Will caught sight of something out of the window.

"It's my grandson! He's lost out there, walking around, and asking for help." Said Will in bemusement. "I can't see him well, but his eyes look funny. I got to go!"

At once, before John could reply to him, Will grabbed the ax and ran back to the window to break it down.

"Wait, Will! There's no one out there!" Yelled John while trying to hold the burly man back.

"He's right there!" Screamed Will. "Open your eyes!"

John tried using as much rationale on him as humanly possible, that, although he too saw the boy, the figure could not have been his grandson. Finally, John was able to pry the ax from him and knock him to the floor. The two men looked at each other for a few moments before John helped him up.

"You took a lot of Xanax, Will. You're probably just hallucinating."

John then lied that he didn't see the boy and it was all in Will's head. It took a while for him to calm down but, after popping two more bars of Xanax, he passed out not too long afterwards.

The sun set about an hour later, and John went to lie beside Mary on the floor for an early bedtime.

"Maybe we should leave." Said Mary, face-to-face with John.

"Do you want to become like them? Like Rick, or the truck driver?" He replied, thinking she was being stupid, but also understanding that they couldn't stay indefinitely.

"I'm just scared." She said. "Nothing is making sense."

John could only comfort her, saying everything will work out and she just needed some sleep. He put his arms around her and, no later than five minutes, she was able to escape the cabin in her head as she dozed off. John, on the other hand, could not sleep. He was essentially carrying the group and the de facto leader, so the burden of fear was most on his shoulders.

For a mysterious and strange reason, as John lay on his side, he got the dreaded feeling that he was being watched–just as before, when he was in the attic looking at the creature. He turned and sat up to see Megan sitting quietly on a couch, chillingly watching him in the darkness.

"What are you doing?" He asked her.

"I can't sleep." She said. "I'd feel much safer if we were in the other house."

John's nerves had gotten the best of him and he didn't know how to respond. Something was wrong about her, and it arose after returning from the woods. He lied back down, ever so slightly keeping one of his eyes open to watch her, while he held a kitchen knife tightly under the sleeping bag.

Chapter 7

Endless Craze

The next toll to be taken was on Pete. He had continued to see himself in the mirror with black irises and began to avoid looking at both himself and others in the eyes altogether. Megan was not helping, ceasing to speak with him (but everyone, in truth), and when bonding was needed most in the dark enigmas that encompassed them, he felt evermore isolated and lonely. He'd frequently sit with his head in his knees and occasionally cry. He was a man, but a young one at that, and not as tough as John and Will—for whom he had no real relationship with. Like John, he avoided sleep whenever he could—only taking gentle and brief catnaps during the daylight.

To throw gas on the fire, Joe continuously harassed the others, insisting that they leave. It was freakish at just how hellbent he was on getting them out of there. He asked Pete if he'd go with him, but the latter man provided no reply. As hours passed, he'd grow even more angry. For whatever reason, after being offered the suggestion, Joe refused to go outside alone. There may have been a deeper, secret reason why he wouldn't, but everyone assumed it was because he was scared. At any rate, the others (besides Megan) still did not wish to head out so soon.

On the subject of he and Megan, John had noticed that she and Joe were spending evermore time with one another, despite neither saying much. Megan would always sit closely beside him at every chance she had; entirely forsaking Pete and his grief. In fact, anytime Pete attempted to talk with her intimately or even how a friend would, she'd minorly lash out at him and demand that he leave her alone unless "he decided he'd go with her to the other house".

John, who had stayed up all of the previous night, decided to rest on the bed in a back bedroom and take a nap. Suddenly, about two hours later, he awoke to loud shouting.

Running into the living room, he discovered everyone backed into a corner, held at gunpoint by Joe with Will's rifle. He commanded that everyone pack up their things and they'd leave together. Oblivious to the fact that John was in the room, John snuck up beside him and punched him square against the side of his head, swiftly knocking him out.

Joe came to his senses roughly five minutes later to find Will holding the gun at him from a chair he was sitting in. Slowly getting to his feet, Joe apologized for lashing out, excusing himself for his anger and blaming it on fear and desperation. Already exceedingly skeptical of the mystery man, Will and John both vowed to never take their eyes off of him from then on, but still understood the man's plight and fright.

"You're not leaving this living room. Understand? You're going to get less food than the rest of us for that." Will said to him.

Joe simply nodded.

John then headed to the attic to again take the role of a guard, asking Mary if she'd join him. The sight of the outside world was the same and unchanged above. The blizzard still wouldn't let up and the fog seemed to get thicker and thicker. As the two sat there looking out of the window, they recounted their regrets in life—the divorce, in particular.

Infidelity had nothing to do with it, which is usually the case. Their love was once burning and their hearts, inseparable, but as the years passed on, they had begun to talk less and less, with both losing interests in both their daily activities and with each other. They were growing old and, for whatever reason, also growing out of their former selves and passions.

They promised, although extremely unlikely, that if they got out, they'd never go through with it. Even more than marriage, was their thought of their daughter. They could only pray that she was safe from the evil that was occurring and that the whole world wasn't affected. They'd never know.

"I'm going to go get some wine." She said.

Only moments later after her departure, John heard her crying out in distress. Immediately and without an iota of hesitation, John tripped as he sprinted down to the living room. He first saw Mary in tears with her hands over her mouth when, turning the corner, he was horrified to see Megan on her knees, holding a knife through Pete's right eye.

Without thinking, Will went straight to his rifle and pointed it to her. Now, her eyes were even blacker than before.

"What the hell are you!?" Yelled Will.

"We just need to get out of the cabin." She said, before running to him.

In an instant, Will pulled the trigger. She staggered a bit, yet oddly did not fall. Again, a shot rang out, only to result in another stagger. He shot two more times—the last in the head—before she finally fell dead. Her blood flooded the floor, just as black as her eyes.

Joe then started to laugh hysterically.

"It won't do any good to kill each other." He said. "You really think they won't get in here, one way or another?"

"Tie this bastard up!" Will said to John. "Whatever or whoever this freak is, he's not natural."

John soon did so after bashing Joe against the head, leaving him passed out.

"What's happening?" Said Will, still in shock and paralyzed.

The three could only look at each other, speechless and traumatized. Will went straight for the liquor, guzzling down whiskey as fast as he could. Meanwhile, Mary continued to cry and hug John fiercely. There were now only four left; maybe three...

"Help me, Will." Said John, as they dragged the body and yet again tore open the door to throw her outside.

Will nearly drank himself to death in shame and guilt, continually vomiting and falling while John paced around the room, holding his head and contemplating on what to do next.

An hour later, the body of Megan had disappeared from the snow, as did her blood.

Chapter 8

Mystery Grows

John and Mary remained in the attic for the remainder of the day; partly because of paranoia and wanting to avoid being down below, and partly to scout outside for any more potential threats.

John was looking through his binoculars when he appeared to catch a glimpse of two figures walking to the house. He handed the device to Mary to let her get a look too, making sure he wasn't the only one able to see them, when she commented that both looked like Joe, wearing the same outfits.

They couldn't get a proper look at any of their features, only the suits, and found them walking straight to the door, until the two heard a knock. There was no way either of them were letting in any more visitors, but they decided to go down and get a better look. Through the downstairs window, they noticed the two were strikingly similar to Joe. They were absent of any hair and had pleasant expressions on their faces; not to mention their black eyes.

John went to the door and asked who they were from behind it.

"We're looking for a place to stay." One said. "We've become lost in this fog and our car got stuck."

"We're not letting anyone in." John said in a stern voice.

"We cause any trouble nor impose." They said. "We just need shelter."

John was beginning to get bolder and demanded they leave at once.

"Go away or I'll shoot you." He exclaimed.

"Very well." Said one of the men.

Despite this, John did not hear them leave and again went to the window. He saw them continuing to stand there; still with grins. He held the rifle tightly in his hands, having grabbed in from a passed out Will. What felt like a lifetime, but was only a mere ten minutes, the two finally departed, quickly disappearing into the fog and snowfall.

"So that's the kind of person you are now?" Said Joe, laughing while bonded to a chair. "Letting poor people die out there and not helping. Obviously they were safe, yet you still refuse to leave."

"Shut it!" Yelled John, having enough of Joe's comments.

John then violently grabbed a chair and moved it to the front of the door, sitting in it while holding the rifle thereby. Two hours passed, when everyone noticeably began to freeze. The stove had not been attended to and all that remained inside of it were dimming coals. Even with blankets, surviving the negative fahrenheit temperatures would be slim. He knew he'd have to get wood, with nothing left to burn.

He was glued to the door, afraid to leave, but could never ask Mary to go outside—even if it was but ten feet to the wood stack. Finally, he forced himself up, and prepared to walk out quickly. It was dangerous, but not nearly as far as he'd gone out last time. Will was slowly getting out of bed, still throwing up from a hangover.

"Will," exclaimed John, "keep an eye out for me."
He said, while handing him back the rifle.

John slowly tore open the door and carefully looked around before running to the stack. At the same time, the German shepherd also ran, this one sprinting out into the fog and barking—apparently having caught sight of something. John called out to him, only to see one of the creatures tear open the poor dog.

Will, furious, fired shots at it from inside while John ran through the door. Before he could fully shut and barricade it, the being lunged against it and tried to pry it open. As Mary and Will attempted to push it shut, John grabbed the ax and cut off the hand of it. Surprisingly, it was a good deterrence, and the creature retreated. In a matter of 50 seconds, the door was again secure.

As it leaked black blood on the floor, Will picked it up with salad tongs and threw it in the stove, where it quickly burned.

Finally granted warmth, John, Mary, and Will huddled around the heat when they noticed a foul, pungent, and sweetly-sick smell emanating from the backyard where the wood was. Upon investigating, John looked through a crack where he found the innocent dog skinned, decapitated, and nailed to the wall of firewood. He trembled in his boots and knew whatever it was out there was trying to send a message. Future heat was no longer a possibility. He chose not to tell anyone—especially Will—so as not to trouble them any further. He, however, was more scared than any of them at that point.

An hour later, John was in the bathroom sealing cracks in hopes of better insulating the house, when he heard Will shouting and banging objects. He ran to see Will throwing empty alcohol bottles in anger.

"You took all my alcohol and food! You bastards!" He screamed. "I'm dying here!"

Inside, Will wanted to kick them out, but couldn't bring himself to do it, likely due to a newfound phobia of being alone, or knowing John and Mary would surely die if he did. Joe, on the other hand, he wouldn't be so considerate to if he opened his mouth.

John knew alcohol was his only friend left; it was all he could rely on to get him through the nightmare.

Will then grabbed one of the hammers and began beating it against the window, ordering the creatures to finally "break in and just kill us already!".

John told him to calm down as best he could and it actually, to his amazement, worked. Will threw the hammer across the floor before leaning over the counter and pondering deeply.

"What do we do?" He said. "We're going to freeze or starve—whichever comes first."

"I'll go down to the cellar." John said. "'See if I overlooked anything."

To his dismay, only small jars of spices remained. It was certain: they would die without leaving. However, as fortunate and incidental as it was, he noticed one of the spine-chilling birds perched on a window sill. Slowly, he walked over to it and unsheathed his buck knife. It was the window Joe had broked days before and he'd be able to stab it through the planks of wood.

Once he neared it to a length of only two feet, he swiftly trusted his knife into its torso. The luck he felt before turned sour when the blood leaking from it and on the knife was black. He was heartbroken, knowing he'd never eat such a thing.

"Dammit!" He exclaimed to himself.

He walked back to the living room, looking at Pete's body lying down. It made him sad, as he'd become moderately close to the young man and was braver than most his age. He was relieved to see coagulating dark red blood beside him. Whatever black symbolized, Pete was definitively human.

They were too scared to put his body outside, as well as too dignified to let him be taken by the beings, so wrapped him up as best they could and dragged him into a corner.

To make things worse, they noticed that the mysterious mold outside was infecting everything inside with an exceedingly fast pace. It'd creeped in a while ago, but was now starting to get serious with its toxic fumes penetrating the air. How could mold flourish in such a cold environment? No one would ever know.

"You're all going to die here." Said Joe with a smirk. "Why not at least attempt an escape?"

By this time, the three had wholly started to ignore him—even if he made sense at times. He couldn't be trusted, no matter what.

At one point, Will had rested his hand on the head of a wooden chair before quickly realizing the mold was on it. It didn't seem like a big deal at the time and he thoroughly washed his hands, but, 30 minutes later, his palms began to literally burn and blister. He was tough–the toughest, in fact–but couldn't help but cry in pain. It acted as a sort of acid and started to eat away at his flesh at an alarming rate. They could do nothing but pour melted snow on it, only to see it get ever worse.

They were appalled when his flesh had begun to fall off and expose bones. He screamed at the top of his lungs and John, trained in first aid, could think of no choice other than amputate it. He asked for Will's permission who flatly refused. As the pain got even more excruciating, he finally relented and said yes in a desperate plea.

He set his hand on the counter, where John tied a belt around the wrist as tightly as he could. He then lifted up a butcher knife, prepared to do one of the most revolting actions of his life. He looked attentively at Will–who was drenched in a mix of tears and sweat–when a nod was given and the knife violently thrashed downward.

Will immediately fainted and blood leaked through the wound, but, thanks to John's skills, it wasn't serious enough to be deadly. John dropped to the floor and leaned against the wall, abhorred by what he'd just done. He, like Will, dozed off.

When he awoke, he began coughing terribly and realized the air was becoming too saturated by the moldy fumes. He got up to see Pete's leg (which stuck out of the blanket), being no more than clean bones.

He exclaimed for Will and Mary to get up so they could go up to the attic where the air was likely better. Joe, as usual, sat in his seat, unperturbed and lightly smiling.

They had no choice, as they crammed themselves on the ground and gazed out of the tiny window, to finally accept their fate. Every which way seemed as hopeless as the next. John recalled the snowmobile in the distance.

Riding it seemed to be their only chance at getting

anywhere, but where? Even so, he couldn't imagine actually

being able to reach it; not as the creatures were fixated on

the cabin more than ever.

There was, however, at least one consensus: they'd

rather starve or suffocate than suffer at the claws or teeth of

that which crept outside.

Chapter 9

Safety?

As Will kneeled by the window, looking out with the scope of his rifle, John and Mary prepared molotov cocktails in the rear with oil bottles and one last container of vodka John forgot he left up there. It took all of Will's strength not to fight him for it.

The snow had risen to over ten feet now and, if they were to somehow leave, the only exit would be through the humble circular window.

As they sat in eerie silence, they heard the sound of wood breaking below and things falling. Fearing the beings had finally, once-and-for-all, broken in, they recoiled and prepared their weapons, before deciding to go down and fight. They had no other choice.

John was first to make it. He found the chair that Joe sat in was turned over with the rope sliced apart. More serious, however, was the fact that the front door was open, with the boards having been torn to shreds. The snow in front of it was completely cleared in an instant when Joe must've escaped.

As snowflakes and howling wind blasted into the house, the three scurried to move anything they could to keep the damaged door shut. As Will shuffled a heavy chair over, he saw one of the creatures rushing towards him. Quickly, he pushed the chair in front of it, but the being managed to get his arms through the door.

He held a knife and, over and over again, struck and sliced at the creature, but it seemed to have little effect. Then, as he went for a jab at the creature's face, there was a swift flash of his claw. Will's head fell off in an instant, with his heavy, lifeless body plummeting to the floor.

John was quick to grab the rifle and fire away at it. To his elation and surprise, the beast seemed to have died—or at least become incapacitated. Yet, two more pairs of eyes opened in the far distance outside and John knew neither he nor Mary had the strength to take another one down.

Without so much as a moment's thought, John ran to the cellar and grabbed a can of gasoline.

"Go to the cellar!" He cried, once returning upstairs.

In a hurry, he doused the floor and tables with the fluid and lit them on fire. The home was instantly turned into a pyre and he sprinted (nearly jumped) into the cellar and slammed the door shut.

Abruptly, John and Mary were covered in pure darkness and silence—even more than they were originally. They could only sit and hold one another as the loud sound of crackling wood and beams falling on the surface was heard.

All they could do was wait potentially. With hope, they prayed that the creatures would assume they were dead and leave the area.

About what they could only perceive as two hours, most of the burning had stopped and the noises of flames and crashings had dulled. Then, a voice arose above.

"Mom? Dad? Are you here? I'm trying to find you."

It was their "daughter".

Mary, despite no longer being ignorant of the situation, couldn't help but jump up and want to call back. John immediately grabbed her mouth, explaining to her while whispering that it wasn't her.

"It's a trick." He said, looking into her eyes. "They're trying to find us."

Finally, after calming her breathing, Mary nodded and they sat back down. Finding that the couple was nowhere obvious, whatever was imitating the girl ceased.

They further waited over a day. They were starving and severely dehydrated, but had to be sure the creatures were gone. At last, John decided to slowly look outside.

The door and top of the cellar were obviously destroyed. Their small covering was blocked by a piece of charred plywood, and, with some strength, he gently lifted it up; only but a crack. The fog and snow remained, but, to his delight, he saw no sign of the mysterious beings.

"We got to make a run for it. The snowmobile is our only hope." He whispered, looking down at her.

Again, she nodded.

Slowly and as quietly as possible, the two stepped out into the smoldering wood. It was still incomprehensible, but John vaguely remembered how to get back to the other cabin.

"Don't stop." He whispered, grabbing her by the hand before they made off in a lightning-fast sprint.

They made sure to hold hands the entire way so as not to get separated. As they continued for what seemed like an eternity, John grew very scared that they were lost.

"'You sure this is the right way?" Mary whispered.

John took a minute to get his bearings straight before turning and forcing them to run in another direction. By fate or extraordinary luck, they were infinitely relieved when the cabin approached them.

Immediately, they ran to the garage and began digging the snow out for way of the vehicle. Unexpectedly, they seemed to be entirely safe and for once, free of the beings outside. At last, the snow was cleared and they started the engine. It was, however, at that point when a shriek came from an unknown direction in the distance.

John revved the engine as hard as he could and they made out at high-speed.

Moments later, two creatures, running on all fours, appeared coming up from behind them. Mary took up the rifle and began firing at them. The first three shots were misses, but, on the next, she got one right through the head of one of them, which promptly exploded.

Finally, having had a good do, the rifle ran out of bullets and all that was left in her arsenal were the molotov cocktails. The oil ones failed to explode, no matter how hard she threw, but the vodka one hit the second creature. It didn't seem to kill it; only severely burned, but it thankfully fled in pain.

They were overjoyed as they climbed up a clear hill, knowing they were no longer followed, until they saw the bodies up and to the left of them. It was Megan, Rick, the truck driver, and Joe, standing silently and observing them from afar. Their features could not be made out—save their twinkling countenances and evil, black eyes. For an unknown reason, they didn't chase after the couple, which both found odd.

Increasing their speed even more, they made it to the top of the hill where they saw the road below. Better still, a sight which took their breath away with utter elation, a snow plow with its bright light beams on, was slowly driving down it. Before they continued, however, the valley below caught their attention.

Far down the mountain, occasional gunshots could be heard going off and faint silhouettes of the giant, terrifying, and magnificent creatures with claws were seen. The two sat there for a moment in awe, gaining a feeling of depression and despondence, thinking they'd never escape the blizzard.

At once, John snapped out of it and straight-away headed for the snow plow. He easily caught up with it and signaled for it to pull over. Mercifully, it did.

"Come in. Hurry up!" Said the driver, a skinny man dressed warmly in Winter clothes.

They were more than relieved when the driver looked and spoke entirely normal. There was a passenger in the front seat who simply looked onwards at the road, presumably shaken and scared.

"There's a ski lodge up about a mile. I was radio'd in that the people are secure and safe there. We'll make it in about 15 minutes."

John and Mary leaned back into the backseats, looking at one another and smiling that, for at least another period of time, they'd be safe.

"I didn't introduce you to Mike." Said the driver. "I picked him up not too long ago further down the valley. He says he's been to the lodge too and there's no better place to be."

Then, at that moment, "Mike" turned around with a slight grin to greet the couple. In horror, they noticed his black eyes and lack of hair beneath his hat.

"It's nice to see humans in all of this."